The Day of the Great Wave

The Day of the Great Wave

AND OTHER FOLKTALES

Compiled by the Editors
of
Highlights for Children

Published by Highlights for Children, Inc.
P.O. Box 18201
Columbus, Ohio 43218-0201
Printed in the United States of America.

ISBN 0-87534-618-9

CONTENTS

The Day of the Great Wave

A Japanese folktale retold
by Marcella Fisher Anderson

It is said that long ago a young Japanese boy named Jiro lived near a village by the sea, a tiny village of only 122 people. Around the fish cannery with its tall chimney were all the houses except for Grandfather's little house. His was built beside an old cherry tree, high, high on the mountainside. Jiro lived there with him.

Like all the villagers, Grandfather had relatives on the other side of the mountain. When he went there to visit, Jiro took special care of the little house.

The day before Grandfather was to return from one of his visits, Jiro stepped outside. The air was very hot and heavy. No breeze stirred through the rice fields far up on the mountain. Earthquake weather, Grandfather would say. Just then, the ground trembled a little under Jiro's feet.

Jiro closed the door of the little house. Safely in their places were all of Grandfather's precious possessions, which had belonged also to Jiro's great-grandfather and to his great-great-grandfather.

Jiro started running down the long, steep path to the village, but he stopped suddenly. He stared at what he saw. All the water in the village harbor was going out, as though sucked up by a monstrous fish. Out went the water beyond the shoreline and the piers, out beyond the fishing fleet and harbor, out, out until only sand and stones and giant weeds were left behind.

Jiro watched the children run to the sand flats to pick up shells they had never seen before. Dogs dashed about, teasing fish left flopping in puddles.

All of the grown-ups were indoors, resting from the day's work or cooking the evening meal.

"What is happening?" cried Jiro aloud. "What could it be?" Then he remembered hearing Grandfather's stories about earthquakes and the terrible tidal waves called *tsunami* that sometimes followed.

"Run! Run! " he shouted through cupped hands to the children below. But the children did not hear him. Jiro took off his wide straw hat and waved it up and down and back and forth. But the children still did not see him.

Now all the water in the sea was out of sight. Miles of sand stretched to the horizon.

Jiro's hands started shaking. The fiery sun went behind a smoke-gray cloud, and Jiro knew what he must do. But how could he? What would Grandfather say?

He opened the door of the little house. Carefully, he carried out a few of his grandfather's most precious possessions. There was not time to carry out everything.

Jiro ran inside again to the earthenware pot filled with charcoal still hot from his morning tea. He hesitated. His eyes filled with tears. Was there no other way?

Quickly, he turned the pot upside down onto the straw floor mats. At first the mats only smoked. Then they caught fire. With a heavy heart, Jiro quickly left the little house that meant so much to his grandfather. Soon the walls of the house were engulfed by a flame that flashed high into the sky. The thatched roof caught fire, too, and made a tall column of smoke. Jiro brushed tears from his eyes.

Down in the village, the children saw the flames. They ran to call their parents.

Up the mountain, past the rice fields, climbed the villagers carrying pots and jugs of water. By the time they reached Grandfather's little house, only glowing embers remained.

The village leader pushed his way through the excited crowd. Red-faced, he stood before Jiro. "Everyone in the village climbed high up the mountain to put out the fire," he said.

"Good," said Jiro.

The village leader's eyes flashed. "Why did the house catch fire? You were left in charge of it. What will your grandfather say?"

Before Jiro could answer, someone shouted, "Look! *Tsunami!*"

A towering wall of water approached from far, far out in the ocean. Slowly at first came this great tidal wave. Then it moved faster. In time it filled the ocean sands and the harbor.

The wave threw fishing boats high into the sky and flung them like toy ships against the mountain. It swept away the piers as though they were bamboo splinters. It dropped gaping sharks and twisting tuna onto the tops of trees.

The villagers shouted and pointed as they saw their houses drowned by the *tsunami.* At last, only one building was left standing—the fish cannery with its tall chimney.

A call reached Jiro's ears. "Jiro!" It was Grandfather's voice.

The wind made a terrible roaring through Jiro's thoughts. What would Grandfather say? Quickly, Jiro walked over to his grandfather and bowed very low in front of him. Grandfather bowed back. When he straightened, his eyes took in the glowing remains of his little house. "I see you could not save all of my precious possessions."

Jiro swallowed. He trembled a little.

"But you have saved something more precious." Grandfather smiled, and his eyes glistened. "You have saved 122 lives. I am very proud of you."

For Jiro it was as though the old cherry tree beside the little house had suddenly blossomed with white flowers on every branch.

From the village came a rushing sound. Everyone turned around. The fish cannery and its tall chimney slid out to sea. The last of the village was gone!

Of course, the people had their rice crop to eat and relatives on the other side of the mountain to shelter them. But they never forgot how Jiro had saved them. They wanted to honor him, so when they rebuilt their homes, they built Grandfather's first. His little house still stands today beside the old cherry tree, high, high on the mountainside.

The Secret of Happiness

By Margery Smith

A long time ago in a faraway village, there lived an old, old man. He was so old that his long white beard stretched almost to his knees. This old man lived high on a lonely hilltop in a small wooden cabin. He rarely made trips into the village; but when he did, the people were always friendly, for the old man was very wise and would help the people with their problems.

One day the old man made a speech to the village people. "You know me well," he began. "I've lived here all my life and have learned many things. But today I have made the greatest discovery of all. Today I have discovered the secret of happiness. My secret is so precious that I must be sure you are worthy of knowing it. So I am only going to tell the one person who proves worthy."

The village people were very excited and began deciding who should learn the secret.

"Pick me!" an old woman cried. "I've never done a wrong deed to anyone in my life."

"Have you ever done a good deed, Miss Simpleton?" a quiet voice asked from the crowd. Miss Simpleton looked very angry and stomped down the street.

"Why not me?" shouted a big fellow from the crowd. "I've always done my best to please, and many a horse I've shod for the good people of this tiny village."

"Yes, and many a Sunday morning you've shod them instead of going to church with your wife and children," replied the old man.

"Gentlemen, please!" a man cried. "We'll never solve anything this way. Let's try to decide just what the old man is looking for and then choose the person we think is best."

And so it began. For three days the village elders thought and talked about their problem. Finally it was announced that they had decided who should go to the old man's cabin. Everyone crowded around to hear.

"The quality needed to be worthy," an elder began, "has been decided. Because God has created all things to be beautiful, beauty must be the best quality in the world. We've picked Rosela because she is the most beautiful girl in the village."

So Rosela stepped daintily up the hill to the old man's cottage. She knocked on the door very lightly and was welcomed by the kindly old man.

"Please come in, child," he said with a smile. "What, pray tell, is on your mind that bid you to climb my long and stony path?"

Rosela spoke sweetly, and her voice was so soft it seemed to float about the room.

"They say I am more beautiful
Than all the stars combined.
And since I am most fair of all,
Your secret I should find."

She stood quietly, waiting for the old man to answer. Rosela was beautiful, but she was also very selfish. So it surprised her when the old man said:

"Beauty is a gift of luck,
Just a false and outward show.
You have no beauty deep inside;
My secret you shall never know."

When the old man said this, Rosela became very angry and stormed back down to the village to report what had happened.

The people were surprised to hear Rosela's story, but they were determined to learn the old man's secret. So for three more days the village elders were at work. Finally, it was announced that another person had been chosen.

"God planted trees and made great rivers so we may grow rich on his gifts," an elder began. "Therefore, wealth must be the greatest quality in the world. Since Mr. Green is the richest man in the village, he should learn the secret of happiness."

So Mr. Green walked heavily up the hill. He reached the door and knocked loudly. The door opened and the kindly old man said, "Please come in, sir. What, pray tell, is on your mind that bids you to climb my long and stony path?"

Mr. Green pulled some coins out of his pocket and grinned.

"I've skimped and saved all my life.
I never spent an extra cent.
Because of my great wealth, I feel
Your secret for me was meant."

The old man looked very sad and said:

"Money is a sort of wealth—
A necessity of life, I guess.
But your money isn't worth the price
To pay for happiness."

Mr. Green glared angrily at the old man and stormed down the hill.

It was the end of the day. The old man was very tired and sad. He was beginning to lose his faith in the village people. Through the window he watched a small girl playing with a bird. He watched the girl awhile and realized she was crying. The old man went into the meadow and asked the girl what was wrong. She looked up and said sadly,

"Excuse me, sir, for coming here
And trespassing on your land.
But I saw this bird—he's hurt his wing.
I think he needs a friend."

The old man smiled and knew he had found the person he was looking for. Watching the little girl holding the bird in her arms, the old man knew that no one can be truly happy unless that person cares about others. Smiling the old man said,

"If you think of others, not just yourself,
You'll finally come to know
That joy and happiness are hidden
In the kindness that you show."

So the old man and the little girl told the people their secret. And from that day on, the little village was the happiest in the land.

The Measuring Chain

By Meg Elbow

In the ancient land of Persia in the days of long ago, there lived a mighty king. He was rich and powerful and known for his terrible temper. Whatever he wanted, he commanded to be done, and he expected to be obeyed instantly.

"Before I die," he announced one day, "I want the most beautiful mosque in all the world to be built in our city."

So he called together the best artists, craftsmen, and builders in the land, instructing them to design and build such a mosque. It should be the biggest and most beautiful building in all the East, faced with brilliant tiles of green and royal blue, and ornamented with mosaics of turquoise, yellow, and gold arranged in intricate design.

Work began. The mosque grew daily until the walls were half-built. Then the master builder assembled his workers and said, "The mosque has reached the halfway point. Now the walls must have six months to settle before we build them any higher. Otherwise, cracks will appear in the mosque when it is finished. So for six months no more work is to be done here."

Now, it was the king's habit to go daily to inspect the building of the mosque. When he found that all the work had stopped, he became very angry and insisted that the master builder be brought before him.

"Why are you not working on the mosque?" he raged at the cowering master builder. "You know I want it finished soon!"

"Your Majesty, forgive us," pleaded the master builder. "I am sure Your Majesty knows that all buildings need six months to settle when they are half-built. Otherwise, cracks will appear when the building is finished; it will be unsafe and its appearance will be ruined."

"Nonsense!" roared the king. "There is not time for this settling. The mosque must be finished soon. You will go on with the building at once!"

"Then, Sire," said the master builder, "will you grant one favor first?"

"What is it?" asked the king.

"I ask for time to forge a chain that will measure the height of the walls thus far, and I humbly beg Your Majesty to be present at the measuring."

The king agreed, and the chain was forged. The measuring began. The king watched as the chain was dropped from the top of the wall until it touched the ground.

"You see, Sire," said the master builder, "the length of the chain is exactly the same as the height of the wall."

"I see," said the king. "What of it?"

"Nothing now, Sire," said the master builder. "I will call my workers together for instructions."

The king departed, satisfied that the mosque would continue to grow. The next day he went as usual to survey the building, but all was quiet. Not a worker was to be seen.

"Bring the master builder before me!" he roared to one of his servants.

The servant hurried away to fetch the master builder. After a while he returned alone to the king.

"Oh, Sire," he said, trembling with fear, "the master builder is not to be found, nor are any of the workers. In the night they all ran away."

The king flew into a terrible rage and ordered all of them to be brought back and put to death. But though his men searched far and wide throughout the kingdom, the master builder and the workers were not to be found.

Six months went by. The half-built mosque stood deserted. Then one day a messenger appeared before the king.

"Your Majesty, I have a message for you from the master builder. He knows that you have ordered him to be put to death when he is found, and he has offered to return if you will grant him one favor."

"What is it this time?" fumed the king.

"He begs that Your Majesty will meet him at the mosque with the chain that was forged before you ordered him to be put to death."

"Very well," said the king.

The king went to meet the master builder and ordered the chain to be brought to the mosque.

"Sire," said the master builder, falling on his knees before the king, "grant your humble servant one more favor. Take the chain and measure its length against the height of the walls. You remember, Sire, that six months ago they were exactly the same."

The king took the chain and commanded his servants to measure the walls with it. The chain fell down the length of the wall and trailed along the ground. It was now much longer than the height of the walls.

"You see, Sire, how much the walls have settled," said the master builder. "You see what big cracks would have appeared if we had continued the building six months ago. Now the settling is finished, and work can begin again if you wish."

The king was dumbfounded. His anger left him.

"You are a wise man, master builder, and a brave one. You have saved my mosque and my pride. Recall your workers and let the building go on. If the mosque is finished before I die, you shall be very well rewarded."

Work on the mosque went forward at full speed. Its walls grew higher and higher, gleaming with colored tiles. Over them rose a golden dome and four slender minarets. Elaborately carved doorways, courtyards with fountains, and intricately patterned mosaics of turquoise, yellow, royal blue, and gold added beauty. At last, all was finished.

The king was delighted. "Truly it is the most beautiful mosque in the world!" he said. "I am happy I have lived to see it finished."

Then, remembering his promise, he sent for the master builder.

"You are a good and faithful servant, master builder. Here is a purse of gold. But I have one last task for you to perform. Take the measuring chain and fasten it over the main gateway of the mosque. Thus will all those who pass through be reminded of the lesson you have taught us."

The master builder did as he was bidden. From that day to this, the mosque still stands, and over the gateway hangs the chain. Through the years, the legend of the chain has been handed down from generation to generation.

The Silkie

A Scottish folktale retold
by Frances Wright-Johnson

Many years ago, on a small Hebridean island off the west coast of Scotland, there lived a silkie—a beautiful being, part human and part seal.

A fisherman and his wife, who lived alone, longed for a child of their own, but their wish was not granted. One evening, when the fisherman was spreading out his nets to dry on the beach after a hard day of fishing in the ocean, he heard a soft crying. He looked around and realized that the crying was coming from farther down along the shoreline. He knew that there were few children who lived nearby, so he was puzzled as to whose child it could be. He walked toward the crying.

On the sand between the rocks he saw a baby seal without its mother, crying like a human baby. The poor creature would die soon if someone did not feed it.

He searched up and down the beach for the mother seal, but he could not see any sign of her at all. So he wrapped the baby seal in his jacket and took it home to his wife, who was waiting at the cottage door.

"Look, Wife, what I found on the seashore! Poor little baby seal has lost its mother. We must feed it so it does not die!"

His wife stared at the baby seal, which was slowly starting to take the form of a baby boy! She was absolutely amazed.

"Oh, Husband," she gasped, "he must be a silkie!"

"We have wanted a child for so long. We must keep this silkie, I think, and care for him and love him as our own baby," the husband said.

They agreed that they would treat him as their son and bring him up as a human being. But they knew that if the boy put as much as his big toe in the ocean, he would turn back into a seal again.

The boy grew up in health and happiness. But his father would never take him fishing, just in case he would get wet with seawater.

When the boy was big enough, he helped on the family's small farm (called a croft in Scotland), where he grew fresh vegetables and tended a small flock of black-faced sheep.

Time went by, and the lad grew up to be bigger than the fisherman. He was tall, lean, and strong.

One winter day, the fisherman was fishing out in the ocean when a terrible storm came up. One by one the other fishing boats from the island made it back to the sheltered bay. The fisherman had gone far out to sea that day, and the little boat was battling its way through the rough sea. Suddenly a heavy, black wave capsized the fishing boat just as it entered the bay.

"Oh, someone help my husband, please," the fisherman's wife begged. But no one was able to brave the rough seas. The villagers watched in horror as the waves pounded the small boat.

From up on the cliffs the silkie saw his father in danger. He had not been in the sea since he was a baby seal, but he knew he had to go to help his father. Without a moment of hesitation, he dived off the cliff into the raging sea below.

The villagers watched in hope and in awe as the young man battled his way through the sea. Instead of tiring, he swam with greater and greater strength. He pulled the old fisherman to safety and left him on the beach. Then the silkie turned and disappeared back into the waves.

The old couple went back to their cottage with heavy and sad hearts. They knew their boy had turned back into a seal and so was lost to them.

When the storm calmed the next evening, the fisherman and his wife went onto the beach again. They heard a strange singing coming from the sea and they knew then that their boy was safe in the sea, in the form of a seal. They went down to the water's edge, and the silkie swam to shore and told them of some of the wonders beneath the ocean waves. He said he would come back once a year to tell them of all the marvelous sights that he had seen. And he always did.

CHALLENGE TO THE KING

By D.J. Chaconas

Long ago there lived a girl named Trinka who had a cow named Clover. Trinka loved Clover with more warmth than the sun could give in a year's time. But now her heart ached. Clover was ill. She looked at Trinka with mournful eyes.

"Oh, my Clover!" Trinka would say. "If I had some gold, I could take you to a doctor." And then Trinka would cry and bury her face in Clover's neck.

As the days passed and Clover did not get better, Trinka decided upon a plan. She would take Clover to the Royal City of the king, where there were many doctors. And although Trinka had no gold, she knew she must try to find a way to find someone who could help cure Clover.

With a rope around the cow's neck, Trinka started slowly on her journey. She had never done such a bold thing before. Would the doctors listen to her? And even if they did, how could she pay them? Trinka didn't know. But she knew that Clover had to get well. For this, Trinka would give anything that was possible for her to give.

The Royal City danced with color and hummed with the music of busy people. Trinka kept herself and Clover as close to the buildings as possible. Her head spun in confusion. How would she find a doctor in this big, busy city?

A messenger of the king suddenly stepped in front of Trinka. He nailed a scroll to the wall beside the girl. No sooner had he done this than a crowd began to gather.

The announcement read "I, King Ustellante, call forth anyone who dares to challenge my talent, my strength, my skill, my wisdom. Let anyone come forth and I shall meet him or her. The person who can defeat me shall be granted any wish that is in my power to give."

"But who can defeat great King Ustellante?" a woman asked. "He is stronger and wiser than any ten men in the kingdom!"

"And more proud than twenty!" another answered. "If it weren't for his pride, he could be a good king."

"The person who can defeat me shall be granted any wish . . ." The thought went through Trinka's head again and again. Certainly a king would have the best doctors—doctors who could cure Clover.

"But in what way could I challenge the king?" wondered Trinka. "I am not wise or talented."

Even so, Trinka found herself following the people to the palace courtyard. She stayed behind the crowd with Clover and stood on tiptoe to see. There was the king! The first challenger of the day was a talented singer. But King Ustellante sang with such feeling that the women started to weep, and then the men wept, too.

The next challenger showed his strength by lifting two full-grown men. But King Ustellante, with his proud smile, won the challenge by lifting three.

Then a great scholar questioned the king. But the king gave wise and learned answers to the questions.

Hearing the king's wisdom, an idea came to Trinka. In her excitement, she called out without thinking, "Can you cure my cow?"

Suddenly, the courtyard became quiet. Everyone turned to Trinka, who was now trembling with fear.

"What is your challenge, little country girl?" the king asked.

Trinka stammered, unable to answer. Then she felt Clover's nose rubbing her shoulder. It gave her a moment of courage, and she spoke out, "Can you cure my cow?"

At first the king laughed. But then he roared in such an angry voice that Trinka thought her legs would fold under her.

"What kind of challenge is that?" the king demanded. "Is it a challenge at all?"

"No!" the Royal Court said. "It is not a challenge unless the girl herself has the power to cure the poor cow."

"Well? Do you?" bellowed the King.

Trinka shook her head.

"Then take yourself and your cow out of here!" the king roared. And with that he gave Clover's tail an angry slap.

The cow jumped, and Trinka spun around. All her fear turned into anger against anyone who would hurt her Clover.

"You would hurt a cow that is ill?" Trinka shouted. "Have you no honor? No decency?"

"Is that a challenge?" the Royal Court asked.

"Yes!" Trinka answered. "I challenge His Majesty to apologize!"

A shocked silence filled the courtyard. The whole Royal Court looked to the king.

"I won't apologize to this country girl!" the king said. "And I won't apologize to a cow!"

"But, Your Majesty," the Royal Court said, "*it* is a challenge. If you cannot do it, you will lose."

The king's eyes blazed. His face turned deep red in his fury. But he could not say the words. Finally he turned away from Trinka, unable to look into the girl's eyes any longer.

A cheer went up from the people. "The little country girl has won!"

A moment passed before Trinka understood their cheers. And then a great shock of joy passed through her.

"Clover, my dear Clover," she cried, "I can have any wish I want!"

The Royal Court led the girl and the cow into the palace to King Ustellante, who no longer wore a proud smile.

"And what is your wish?" the king asked, his voice suddenly quiet. "Do you wish half my kingdom?"

Trinka shook her head. "I wish only that my cow, Clover, be cured. I want her to be well again."

"And that is all?" the king asked, surprised.

Trinka nodded. Then there was a long silence.

"Your wish shall be granted," said the king. Then he added with a smile, "And I apologize to you and your cow."

Ungrateful Anna

retold by Irene Stack

Once, long ago, in a land far away there lived an old woman called Anna. She lived with her good husband, Vladir, on the rolling green hills of their small but comfortable farm. They had two cows, one goat, ten chickens, one rooster, three pigs, a strong horse, and an old dog named Schmootz.

Anna should have been very happy. Not only did the farm produce enough for them to eat, but they were able to sell several bushels of vegetables, a few dozen eggs, and enough milk to earn some money besides. But still Anna was not a happy and cheerful person.

"What makes you so unhappy, Anna?" asked her good husband, Vladir.

"Why should I be happy?" cried Anna. "I work hard all day in our small house. It is so small that I have no room for the many dishes, the stacks of linen, and all the silverware. And, if that is not enough, there is all the food that you bring home that I must cook."

"If you are troubled," said Vladir comfortingly, "then go to see Alix, the wisest man in the village. He will advise you. Meanwhile, I will store your dishes, fold your linen, and clean your silverware. But alas, dear wife, since I cannot cook, I must leave that chore for you."

Instead of thanking Vladir, Anna sighed a huge sigh. "Oh," she wailed. "I should be tired to death if I were to walk."

"Then take our strong horse and you will not be so tired," offered Vladir.

"If I were to take our horse, I would have to put on his harness and hitch him to the buggy. Surely I would have no strength left to go see the wise Alix."

"Then I will harness the horse and hitch him to the buggy for you, dear Anna."

Instead of thanking her kind husband, Anna said, "Oh, I shall be so lonely on that long trip. What shall I do?"

"Then take our dear old faithful dog, Schmootz," suggested Vladir.

Ungrateful Anna climbed into the buggy, and Vladir whistled for Schmootz. When they were all set in the buggy, he handed the reins to Anna. He called to the horse, "Kl, kl, kl! Go, boy, and take Anna and Schmootz to see Alix, the wise one." Then he went about doing his farmwork and Anna's housework as well.

It wasn't long before Anna stepped out of the buggy with Schmootz yelping at her skirts. An old man with a tangle of gray beard stood at the doorway of a low wooden house with a grass roof. His hair was rumpled. He wore an old sweater with many patches and a striped woolen muffler wrapped several times around his neck. "Halloo, Anna," he called. "Why do you come to see poor Alix?"

"Alix, oh, wise one," pleaded Anna, "you are the only one who can help me."

"Are you in some terrible trouble, old woman?"

"It seems terrible enough to me." Saying this she shooed Schmootz out of the way and sat down.

Alix put an old soupbone at the doorway for Schmootz and offered Anna a glass of tea. "Come, dear Anna, tell me what is your terrible trouble?"

"My work gets harder and harder every day," the old woman moaned. "It won't be long before I work myself to the bone. The house is so small that I work hard at putting all my dishes away. It takes the entire morning to fold all my linen, and it takes forever to clean my silverware. I hardly have time to cook the food I have in the house. Tell me, Alix, oh, wise one, what can I do?"

Alix looked at the foolish woman before him and mumbled to himself. "I have but one bowl, one glass, and one spoon. Lord knows when there will be enough food in my house to feed myself, let alone the good people who visit me. This woman does not know that her lot is a good one." Then he spoke, "Anna, go and take your two cows into the house. Then come and tell me if your house is still small and your work is still too hard."

Anna was horrified at this. But since Alix was a great wise man, she did not question his word. She did as she was told and returned the next day, saying, "Oh, wise one, my house is smaller than ever and my work harder still."

"Then go home," commanded Alix, "and bring your goat into your house as well. Come back when you have done this."

Anna could not understand the advice, but she followed it. With each passing day, the wise one, told her to bring more animals into her home until Anna and Vladir were living in their tiny house with two cows, one goat, ten chickens, one rooster, three pigs, one horse, and the old dog, Schmootz.

With all this Vladir simply smiled and said, "If this is what the wise man suggested, then I am content."

But Anna was not content. She was beside herself. "I shall be worked to death trying to keep this house clean with all those animals," she cried. So once more she paid a visit to Alix, the wise one.

This time he advised, "Take your two cows back to the barn and then come to see me."

Anna hurried home and happily took the cows back to the barn. She returned to Alix and told him that she had done as he had asked.

"Now," questioned the old man, "do you have more room in your house?"

"Well," replied Anna, "it is a little better."

"Then go home and turn the goat out to pasture." Once more Anna was eager to obey and did just as Alix suggested.

"Now," asked the wise man, "is there more room in your house?"

"Oh yes!" replied Anna.

Alix sent Anna home each day to let one more animal out of the house. Each time she would return to him and tell him that the house had more room and the work was getting easier.

At last all the animals had been turned out of the house. Anna made her last trip to Alix.

"My house has more room than I can remember," said Anna very happily. "Without those animals inside, I can keep everything clean. Now I have lots of time to do all the things I have to do." As she was saying these words, Anna realized how foolish she had been. She was fortunate to own many things and have much food. Instead of being grateful, she had complained.

She gave Alix a basket of food she had prepared and thanked him warmly. Then she returned to her small house and her two cows, one goat, ten chickens, one rooster, three pigs, one strong horse, and her faithful old dog, Schmootz.

Now for the first time she hummed happily as she wiped the dishes, folded the linen, cleaned the silverware, and prepared dinner for herself and her good husband, Vladir.

Li Ching, Rainmaker

A Chinese folktale retold
by Bernadette P.N. Lee Shih

Li Ching was a warrior who lived many, many years ago in China. As a young man, Li was fond of hunting. Every year he went to the mountains, where he would stay in a little village in a valley. As years went by, Li and the villagers became friends.

One day, when Li was returning to the village, he saw a fine stag on the hillside. Li spurred his horse on after the stag, which sped away along a high ridge. He followed the stag into a wooded valley. There, among the thickets, the stag disappeared.

It was dark, and soon Li was hopelessly lost in the woods. The silence was broken only by the mournful howl of a monkey. Li shivered with fear. He dismounted and walked on. Suddenly, he saw a warm light glow in the distance. Li ran toward the light, and to his surprise he saw before him a large house surrounded by high walls. The door was lacquered red and shone in the light of a bright bronze lantern.

Frantically, Li pounded on the door. For a long time there was no answer. Just as Li was about to leave, the door swung open and a servant appeared.

"Can you give me shelter for the night?" Li asked. "I was hunting on the hillside and lost my way in the woods."

"Both my masters are away," the servant said. "Only the Old Lady is home."

"Please give the lady my respects and ask her if she would please give me shelter for the night," Li pleaded with the servant.

At first, the Old Lady was unwilling, but at last she consented.

Li was given a delicious dinner that consisted of various kinds of fish. Then servants brought bedding—sheets and pillows, all soft and clean. However, when the servants left Li's room, they locked his door on the outside.

Although he was very tired, he was unable to fall asleep. He was puzzled. "Who are these people who live in such a big mansion in the middle of the forest?" Li wondered. "Why do they eat nothing but fish? And why is the door to this wonderful bedroom locked on the outside?"

As Li sat thinking on the edge of his bed, he heard a voice roar from outside the gate: "This is a command from on high. The master is to deliver rain over a radius of seven hundred miles!"

The Old Lady replied: "Neither of my sons is home. And none of the servants can undertake such a task. Yet I will be punished if rain is not delivered! What am I to do?"

One of the servants suggested that Li Ching should fulfill the command. The Old Lady was delighted with the servant's suggestion, and she said to Li Ching: "I must tell you that this is not a house of mortals, but an enchanted palace. We are responsible for delivering rain to earth. I have just received an order. Will you help us tonight?"

"I am only an ordinary man," Li Ching replied. "I am a good horseman, but I have no experience riding the clouds. However, since you have been kind to me, I should like to help. If you will show me what I have to do, I will try my best."

Immediately, a piebald horse was led forward. Fastened to the horse was a tiny rain jar.

"You will not need to use reins or whip, Li Ching," the Old Lady began. "Simply let the horse have its way. Whenever it stops and neighs, you must shake one drop of rain from the jar onto its mane. Be sure you use no more than one drop each time."

And so Li Ching mounted and set out on his mission. The piebald horse rose steadily into the air, and soon Li was traveling above the clouds. Beneath him, lightning flashed and thunder rolled. Several times the horse stopped and neighed. And each time Li did as he was told. Whenever he dipped his finger in the jar and shook one drop of water onto the horse's mane, the clouds opened beneath him. Finally, the horse stopped above the little village near the mountains where Li stayed while he hunted.

"The people of this village are my friends," Li said to himself. "For weeks there has been no rain here, and all the crops are dying." And so this time Li shook not one drop but twenty drops of rainwater on the horse's mane.

Li Ching and the horse returned quickly to the dragon palace. To Li's astonishment, the Old Lady was weeping. "Why did you not do as I said?" the Old Lady scolded. "One drop from the rain jar causes three inches of rain on earth. That poor village by the mountains! Flooded out in the middle of the night by five feet of rain."

Li Ching was so filled with sadness by the consequences of his act that tears welled up in his eyes.

Noting Li's remorse, the Old Lady comforted him. "You are not to be blamed, Li Ching, because you are only a mortal and could not be expected to master the art of rainmaking. But my sons will never forgive you for what you have done. So you had better leave at once."

Before Li left, the Old Lady gave him a bag full of large, flawless pearls.

Li looked back when he had ridden a short distance from the palace, but the house was gone. There was no sign of it anywhere.

Dawn came. Li found his way to the village near the mountains. He was heartbroken when he saw the whole village flooded by five feet of water. Fortunately, Li had been clumsy and slow in taking the raindrops from the rain jar. And so the people had time enough to escape up the hillside.

Li rode off to sell the pearls the Old Lady had given him. He used the money to buy food for the villagers until the flood receded, and then he built a new village where the old one had stood.

The whole village rejoiced and thanked Li Ching. He later became a great general whose fame was known throughout China.

Hodja-din Visits a Friend

A Turkish folktale retold by A.A. Howe

It was twilight, but Hodja-din still toiled in his fig orchard. He was proud of his trees, and his careful attention to the fruit assured him of a bountiful harvest. Suddenly, Hodja-din paused in his work.

"Verily," he said aloud, "only now do I remember."

What had entered Hodja-din's thoughts was a reminder that he had been invited to a banquet to be given that night by his friend Selim Kadri.

Quickly, because he was very late, Hodja-din laid aside his tools and hurried down the road. When he reached his friend's house, he found that all the other invited guests had already arrived.

"Good evening," Hodja-din called. But his friend and host, Selim Kadri, seemed not to hear.

Hodja-din was perplexed. He moved about the room, but no one seemed to pay any attention to him. This was strange indeed, he thought, because all of the people here were his friends. When he saw Jelal talking to Ahmed, he walked over to them. But the instant he arrived, both men turned their backs to him.

Hodja-din tried a bit of conversation. "Fazil, your field of barley will yield a good harvest this year."

Fazil acted as if he hadn't heard a word.

Hodja-din tried again. This time he spoke to his host. "Selim, that is excellent fruit you have in your vineyard this year."

Selim also seemed not to hear.

Hodja-din looked over the well-groomed guests and realized that the dust of the field still clung to his garments. He rushed out of the house and hurried home.

After he had scrubbed and washed himself, he dressed in his finest attire and returned to his friend's banquet.

Selim Kadri, the host, greeted him with a bow. "Good evening, Hodja-din. Welcome to the banquet, my friend."

"Thank you," Hodja-din replied, smiling.

Then Jelal joined Hodja-din and bowed. "I've seen your orchard," he said respectfully. "You should have a fine fig harvest this year."

Everyone was pleasant and courteous to Hodja-din now. And as they sat down to eat, Selim Kadri personally filled his plate.

Then, while all watched, Hodja-din carefully picked up the choicest piece of meat on the plate. But instead of putting it in his mouth, he put it in the pocket of his coat, "Eat, coat. Eat." he said.

And as all gazed in astonishment, Hodja-din kept feeding his coat. Pilaf, cheese, pickles, and figs followed the meat into the coat.

The guests stopped eating and stared in disbelief. Finally Selim Kadri, the host, could contain himself no longer. "Tell me, Hodja-din, what do you mean by telling your coat to eat?"

"Why, surely you must wish the coat to eat," Hodja-din replied with an innocent look in his eyes. "For, when I came in my old dirty clothes, there was no place for me. Now, when I come in my fine clothes, nothing is too good for me. That shows it must have been the coat, not me, that you invited to your banquet."

Water for the Chief

An African folktale retold
by Eleanor E. Ullmann

Once upon a time the Chief of the Faraway Forest gave a banquet to which he invited all the denizens of the forest. After much feasting and dancing, the Chief called his wife and said, "A great thirst consumes me. I must drink of the spring that runs into the pool on the other side of the plain. Who will go and bring me water?"

Antelope came forward and said, "Live, O Chief! I excel in speed. I shall bring water to you. Only command me."

Whereupon the Chief said, "Go," and his wife handed Antelope the gourd. Away Antelope went, bounding through the forest and across the plain, and at last he came to the pool of crystal bright water. Stooping down, he began to fill the gourd. As the water was running into it, Antelope espied something bright and shining sitting on the other side of the pool. It was a tiny frog. Antelope was fascinated by its color and stunning beauty. There he sat, forgetful of the great thirst his Chief endured, and so the sun went into the west.

The Chief, unable to endure longer, called for another volunteer, whereupon Lion offered his services. The Chief accepted them, and Lion then bounded through the forest. Upon reaching the pool, he began to reprimand Antelope for his negligence and forgetfulness.

Whereupon Antelope said, "But look, my dear friend, look! Have you ever seen anything so wonderfully beautiful?"

Lion, casting his eyes to the other side of the pool, saw the little green frog, and he also was fascinated by its beauty and color.

Spellbound, he forgot his Chief and his desire to drink of the spring.

The Chief, weary of waiting for Lion to return, called again for a volunteer. This time Leopard sprang forth with his gourd to bring his master a drink. But he also came under the spell of the little frog with bright eyes and green coat. Elephant followed soon after, and then Rhinoceros; and they, too, were held by the beauty of the frog.

In desperation the Chief called again for someone to go and bring the water, but there was little response on the part of the other animals of the forest. They, fearing some terrible calamity had befallen all of the others, refused to go.

Just then Little Tortoise came waddling along, clapping his hands, and said, "Live, O Chief! I know that I am small and that I have no great speed. But give me the privilege of bringing my lord and master water from the spring. I humble myself before thee. Grant me this favor."

The Chief was angry and commanded him to be off, but Little Tortoise pressed his service upon the Chief, saying again, "Give me just this one opportunity of serving thee, and I will bring the water."

Reluctantly the Chief said, "Go!"

Off went Little Tortoise, waddling through the tall grass, climbing over the logs, until he came at last to the pool. There he found his fellows, sitting spellbound by the strange and alluring beauty of the little frog.

On seeing the Tortoise, all with one voice said, "Oh, Little Tortoise, just look at this wonderful frog!"

But Little Tortoise refused to look saying, "My master awaits water. You have failed him. I refuse to look at this frog."

And filling his gourd with water, Little Tortoise went off, waddling his way back to the Chief. The Chief, surprised beyond measure, drank and was thoroughly satisfied.

Then he gave Little Tortoise a special place in his household, saying, "Although you are small and slow-moving, you have indeed a true and faithful heart, and you have proved your respect and love for me."

And so the wise ones of the forest say today that, although you may be very small and very slow, you can be of great service, even to a very great person.

The Three Wishes

A Swedish folktale retold by Ann Stacey

Long ago there lived a poor farmer and his wife. Their farm was but a few acres of rocky land near the river and a range of hills heavy with pine and scrub, but they worked hard and were content with their small successes. They were simply grateful for good health and for each other.

Late one winter evening there came a knock on their door. The farmer swung it open and found three men curiously dressed in tall peaked hats and flowing robes.

"We are on our way to the king's palace," they said. "But we still have a long way to go. May we spend the night with you?"

"Come in, come in," said the farmer. And he and his wife set about at once to try to make their guests comfortable. The visitors were given a hot supper—a simple meal, but the best the wife could provide. The farmer piled wood on the fire until it leaped high, warming and cheering the humble cottage.

After the three guests had finished their meal, the farmer's wife brought out her best homespun linen sheets and warmest handmade quilts. Then, assured of their visitors' comfort, the couple wished their guests good night and retired to the frosty loft where they spent the night.

In the morning the visitors were gone.

It was Sunday, and the farmer and his wife hitched their little pony to the sleigh and went over the ice of the river to church. After the service they mentioned to their neighbors the visit they had had the night before. But after some time had passed, the farmer and his wife forgot about it.

Winter passed, spring came, and many unusual things came about on the little farm. As the snow melted in the sun, all the rocks on their land seemed to melt with it. Soon a long, broad field was left along the banks of the river.

The astonished farmer began at once to plow the field and plant his grain. And it seemed that no sooner were the kernels in the rich soil than the little shoots appeared.

As spring became summer, people came from all over the countryside to see this field where the wheat grew taller than a man.

Meanwhile their one cow had produced twin calves, a beautiful pair of heifers. And though never before a good milker, the cow now gave a full bucket each night and morning and continued to do so right through the following winter.

Their little flock of hens hatched broods of a dozen and more chicks each, so that the farmer was obliged to build a new henhouse to shelter the great flock.

Then one day when the farmer was in the woods gathering firewood for the coming winter, he found the scrub in the hills had somehow been cleared away, leaving valleys deep in meadow grass. Instead of the one solitary cow he had kept for years, the farmer now saw the possibility of keeping a herd and perhaps one day even running a dairy.

The farmer and his wife could scarcely believe their good fortune. After so many years, they had suddenly become prosperous.

Not everyone was delighted by the farmer's newfound success. Directly across the river lived a neighbor who watched his old friend's progress with suspicion and envy. He himself owned a large farm, well established, with a great house and greater barns. His many granaries were always filled at harvesttime, and his sleek cattle dotted the countryside for miles around.

But for all his wealth, he begrudged the prosperity that had miraculously blessed his neighbor. "How had it come about?" he wondered. He decided it could only have been accomplished by the help of the rich visitors the farmer had told him about the previous winter. They must have left him a bag of gold for his simple hospitality.

While the rich farmer stewed with resentment, summer passed; and soon another winter had settled over the countryside. Late one night a knock came at the door of the big farmhouse. There were the three curiously dressed men in tall peaked hats and flowing robes.

"May we find shelter with you?" they asked the rich farmer. "We are on our way to the king's palace but still have a long way to go."

How excited the farmer was! He brought them into his parlor and settled them in the softest chairs. Then he rushed to waken his wife, who immediately set about preparing a rich meal—a stuffed goose that took hours to roast, a steamed pudding that had been intended for the next Sunday dinner, pots and bowls of creamed vegetables and stewed fruits. How she worked! By the time the visitors sat down to this magnificent meal, they were so tired they could scarcely keep their eyes open.

After they had eaten, the farmer ushered them to the guest rooms. And when he finally retired, it was not to sleep but to restlessly speculate on what his vast reward would be.

The first signs of stirring came with the break of day. The farmer was up and ready to greet his honored guests.

"Yes," they said, "we have rested well. No, we have no time for breakfast. We must be on our way. We still have far to go."

"But," they said, "you have been very kind to us. As a token of our appreciation, the next three wishes you or your wife make will be granted."

Without waiting to say farewell, the farmer rushed back to tell his wife.

Three wishes! Oh, what should those wishes be? What did they want that they did not already have? It was a great problem, the farmer and his wife discovered, as they argued back and forth throughout the day. The farmer could not decide between more land or more cattle, or whether to wish for both. The wife was torn between her desire for a diamond necklace and the necessity of owning an ermine coat.

"Another fur coat!" stormed the farmer. "I wish you had been born with fur so that you'd stop all this talk of fur coats, once and for all!"

No sooner had he spoken than, to his horror, his wife turned into a large white weasel.

"You beast!" she screamed to her husband when she saw what she had become. "How I wish you didn't have a tongue in your head!"

And so it happened! The farmer was speechless. No more wishes for him!

There was now but one wish left, and only the wife could make it. "Oh," she sobbed, "how I wish we had never wished for anything but had been happy with our own good fortune."

This turned out to be the best wish of all. The farmer regained his tongue, the wife lost her resemblance to a weasel, and for once they became truly, truly content.

How the Northland Got Daylight

A legend of the Far North adapted
by Christine Malagodi

Ages ago when the world first began, there was no daylight in the Northland. It was dark all the time. As you might imagine, this confused the people. No one knew when it was time to go to bed or when it was time to get up.

In one small village there lived a wonderful crow. The Eskimo people of the village loved him and thought him very wise. Twice a year the crow would fly away on a long journey to distant lands. When he returned, he would visit families in their sealskin huts and, by the light of a seal-oil lamp, tell of all the wonderful things he had seen and done.

After one of his journeys, the crow had something special to tell. "The people in distant lands have daylight," he said.

"What is daylight?" asked the people.

The crow explained. "If we had daylight, we would be able to see a bear that was many yards away, and we would be able to see the fish swimming in the water."

Of course the people thought this was wonderful, and they asked the wise crow if he could bring daylight to their land.

"That would be a difficult thing to do," said the crow. "I know where it is, but I'm afraid I could never get it here."

"But you are such a wise crow," the people said. "You have wonderful, magical ways. Surely you can do it."

"Well," said the crow, greatly flattered by their faith in him, "I will try."

So the next day the crow started on his journey. He flew on and on in the dark for many days. As he flew farther and farther, the sky became brighter and brighter until finally it was flooded with light.

As he perched on a branch of a tree to rest, he looked about him. He saw that the great light came from one of the snow huts in the village spread before him.

By sitting very still and watching, the crow discovered that the village chief lived in that snow hut. And when he saw the chief's wife go to the river to fetch water from the ice hole, he knew that it was time to use some of his wise, magical ways. He slipped out of his crow skin and left it hanging on the limb of the tree. Quickly, he ran to the door of the snow hut and whispered these magic words:

Ya-do-ty, ta-da-ty, ha-ka-ty-o,
Make me so little
That I won't show,
Just as big as a speck of dust
For enter that snow hut, I must.

He then hid on a sunbeam near the door and waited. When the chief's wife came back from the river, the crow, who looked like nothing but a speck of dust, stuck himself to her dress and passed with her into the hut.

Inside, the hut was very bright and sunny. On the floor on a skin of a great white polar bear, a baby played happily with his toys. There were tiny dogs and little walrus heads, foxes, polar bears, and kayaks, all carved out of walrus tusks. The chief sat with the baby, watching him play.

The mother picked up the baby, and a tiny speck of dust drifted from her dress into the baby's ear. The speck of dust, of course, was the crow.

The baby began to cry. "What is it you want?" asked the chief.

The crow whispered into the baby's ear, "Ask for the daylight to play with." And the child did.

His mother removed a small wooden box from the chief's hunting bag and took out a shining ball. The baby played with the ball a long time.

The crow was growing impatient. He wanted to get that daylight ball. Again he whispered in the little one's ear. "Ask for a string to tie to the ball."

The chief tied a string to the daylight ball.

Now the crow had to get rid of the chief and his wife. A third time he whispered in the baby's ear. "Pretend that you are very sleepy."

The child started yawning and rubbing his eyes. The chief and his wife saw that the baby was tired, so they laid him on the polar bear rug, covered him with a sealskin blanket, and tiptoed out of the house, leaving the door open.

As the baby played with the shining ball, it rolled and stopped right in front of the open door.

"Now is my chance," said the crow. He jumped out of the baby's ear and quickly flew back to the tree where his skin was hanging and whispered these magic words:

Ya-ka-ty, ta-ka-ty, na-ka-ty-o,
Make me big so I can go,
Strong wings so I won't fall.
I must get that shining ball.

And then the crow was himself again. He flew into the house, seized the string in his beak, and away he flew.

Flying back was even more difficult for the crow. The daylight ball dangling on the string was heavy. But he kept flying and flying. His wings ached. And he was very tired.

"I know what I can do," thought the wise crow.

As he passed over the first dark village, he scratched some of the daylight from the ball with his claw. The brightness fell on the village below and lit it up beautifully. Then at every village he came to, he did the same thing, and the ball became less heavy and easier to carry.

When at last he reached home, he hovered over the village and scattered the daylight all around.

The people shouted with delight and danced and sang. They had a wonderful party for the crow. They blew out their seal-oil lamps because they now had daylight, and then they sat around the crow.

"If I could have brought all the daylight," he told them, "it would never be dark, even in the winter. But it was just too heavy for me to carry." Then he brightened. "By making the shining ball less heavy, I gave many villages daylight."

So now the people of the Northland have daylight in the summer, and it is still dark in the winter. But that is just fine with the people who until now had never had any daylight at all.

Ivan the Fool

A Russian folktale retold
by Alexander Kucherov

Once upon a time there was a rich man who had three sons. The two older sons were big and strong. They loved only to laugh and to have a good time with friends. The youngest son, named Ivan, was frail. He did not like the noisy company of his brothers. He preferred to go on long walks by himself or sit under the shade of a tree, so he could think his own thoughts and dream his own dreams. Because of that, people thought him strange and called him Ivan the Fool.

One day the rich man died. In his will he had ordered that all of his riches should be divided equally among his three sons.

The two older brothers told Ivan, "Here is your share. As you see, it's quite a bit."

Ivan thought a while and replied, "Thank you, my brothers, but what will I do with all that money? Keep it for yourselves. I'd rather go and seek my own fortune."

The older brothers smiled to themselves. Not for nothing was their brother known as Ivan the Fool. They divided Ivan's share between them. As for Ivan, he took a walking stick and set out on the open road.

Soon he heard cries in the distance. In the middle of a square stood a man beating a dog. People were watching in horror.

Ivan walked up to the man. "Why are you beating the poor dog?" he asked.

"How can I not beat him?" replied the man. "I'm poor. With the last of my money I bought some meat for myself and my family, and when my back was turned, the dog ate it all."

"That's because he was as hungry as you are," said Ivan. "Instead of beating him, why don't you let me have him?"

"Gladly," said the man. "Good riddance."

Ivan continued on his way with the dog at his side. Presently he again heard cries. In the middle of the square stood a man beating a cat. People were watching in horror.

Ivan walked up to the man. "Why are you beating the poor cat?" he asked.

"How can I not beat him?" replied the man. "I'm poor. With the last of my money I bought some milk for myself and my family, and when my back was turned, the cat lapped it all up."

"That's because he was as thirsty as you are," said Ivan. "Instead of beating him, why don't you let me have him?"

"Gladly," said the man. "Good riddance."

Ivan continued on his way with the dog at one side and the cat on the other.

The sun was setting. All three felt tired and hungry. They sat down under a tree. Ivan had brought some food. He shared it with his two new friends. When they had eaten, the dog wagged his tail and licked Ivan's hand, and the cat purred and rubbed against Ivan's leg. Then all three stretched out and went to sleep.

The following day they resumed their journey. They came to a big farmhouse.

"My friend," said Ivan to the farmer, "do you need a helper? I am looking for work. I have little money left, and we have to eat, my two friends and I."

The farmer looked at the frail young man. "I do need a helper," he said. "But it's hard work, and I'm not sure you can do it."

"Let me try," Ivan pleaded.

The farmer looked doubtful, but he said, "Fine. I'll give you a chance to show what you can do. A few yards from here is a lake. I went boating there yesterday. The weather turned bad, the boat turned over, and my wooden cane with the beautiful carved handle fell into the water. Go retrieve it, and be quick."

With the dog and the cat trotting beside him, Ivan hurried to the lake. It was huge. Floating on the water near the far shore was the cane. To swim across and back would take at least an hour, he thought, and the farmer wanted him to be quick.

Ivan sighed and started to take off his clothes. Just then he heard the sound of a splash. The dog had jumped into the water. Quick as lightning, he swam to the far shore and returned with the cane between his teeth.

Ivan dried the cane in the grass and brought it to the farmer.

The farmer was surprised. "So fast?" he said, wondering. "You must be a better worker than I thought. But I have another task for you. In my garden is a tall apple tree. Take this basket, and bring it back full of apples. And be quick."

With the dog and cat at his side Ivan hurried to the garden. Never had he seen an apple tree so tall. It seemed to reach to the sky. Near the top were lots of beautiful golden apples. To climb that high and pick them would be a long, hard task, he thought, and the farmer wanted him to be quick.

Ivan sighed and got ready for the climb when he heard a scratching sound. It was the cat, darting up the tree with the speed of lightning. Having reached the top, he shook the branches, and the apples came down like golden rain. Ivan gathered a basketful and brought it to the farmer.

The farmer was amazed. "So fast?" he said. "You're a wonderful worker, Ivan. I'll be happy to have you work for me."

Ivan worked for the farmer for several months. With every task he was given, his two friends helped him. And the farmer was very pleased.

But Ivan was beginning to feel restless. He wanted to be back on the road and seek his fortune in other places. He told the farmer so.

"I'm sorry to lose such a good worker," the farmer said, "but I can't hold you back. Come to the barn and collect your reward for your good work."

The farmer showed Ivan two sacks—a big one and a small one. "The small sack," he said, "is full of gold coins. The big one is full of sand. Choose either one."

Ivan thought for a while. "What will I do with all that money?" he said. "I'd rather take the big sack with the sand."

That evening the farmer told the story to his wife. She laughed. "What a fool! Imagine—to take a sack of sand when he was offered gold."

"That's what they call him," the farmer said. "Ivan the Fool. Still, he was a kind, hard worker."

Meanwhile Ivan was back on the road, with the dog at one side and the cat at the other and the heavy bag of sand slung over his shoulder.

Before long, the trio heard a voice crying, "Help, help!" They ran to the place where the cries came from. They saw leaping flames. A big house was burning, and a beautiful young girl was crying for help as she struggled to get out the door.

Ivan thought fast. He tore open the big sack and poured the sand on the flames. The flames sputtered and died. The girl was saved.

With tears in her eyes she thanked Ivan for having saved her life. "Do you know who I am?" she asked breathlessly.

"No," said Ivan.

"I am the princess," the girl replied. "My father is the king, the ruler of this land."

Ivan was summoned before the king.

"In gratitude for your courage and your quick thinking," said the king, "my daughter has asked to be your bride, and I have given my consent."

So Ivan married the princess, and they lived happily in the palace forever after. And wherever they went and whatever they did, the dog and cat were at their side.

Throughout the kingdom people said, "Maybe Ivan the Fool is not such a fool after all."

The Gratitude of the Crane

A Japanese folktale retold
by Kimiko Tonogai

This folktale is very popular in Japan. Every child is familiar with it. Stamps have even been issued to commemorate this sad, beloved story.

The old man took a deep breath in the cold air. Snowflakes had been fluttering like butterflies from the morning sky, and now everything was sparkling and silvery in the sun.

Suddenly the man saw something big and white struggling far away under a pine tree. It was a young crane, caught in a trap and desperately struggling for its life.

"Oh, crane, don't move anymore. Be still. I'll set you free."

The old man hammered one side of the trap. He pulled the other side. At last the crane's leg was freed from the trap.

The big white crane rubbed her head again and again against the old man's face. Then she soared high up in the sky.

It snowed all the next day. The old man and his wife sat warming themselves at the fireplace. Suddenly, they heard a knock at the door.

A soothing voice, like a silver bell ringing softly, called, "Hello."

The old man said, "Who can be calling on us in such a storm?"

He opened the door. A very beautiful girl stood shivering in the cold.

"Would you be kind enough to let me stay here overnight?" she said.

"Come in. Come in," said the old man.

"You must be cold. Come here by the warm fire," the old woman called.

The girl knelt down in front of the fireplace and rubbed her hands together.

The old woman poured some millet gruel in a cup for the girl. The old man added more wood to the glowing fire.

The next morning when the old man and woman woke up, the house was already cleaned. Even breakfast was ready. Then the girl came out with a big smile and said, "Good morning." She had brought hot water for them to wash their hands and faces.

It continued to snow. The girl stayed on and took care of the old man and woman. They loved her very, very much.

One day the girl said to the old man and woman, "I don't have any parents. Would you be kind enough to let me stay here forever?"

"We are poor," the old man said, "but we would like you to stay."

"Oh, I am very happy," the girl said. "To thank you, I will weave some pretty cloth for you to sell."

The old man bought many bundles of different-colored thread in town.

When the girl had prepared the loom in the back room, she put a folding screen in front of it. "Please," the girl said, "do not look inside when I am weaving."

The old couple were puzzled, but they promised to do as the girl asked.

For three days the sound of weaving was heard from behind the screen.

On the third day the girl came out with the cloth she had woven.

"I'm finished now," she said, handing the cloth to the old man and woman.

"How beautiful," they said. "It sparkles like a beautiful rainbow."

"Please show this cloth to the lord," the girl said to the old man.

The old man carried the cloth to the lord's palace.

The lord fingered the cloth carefully. Then he said, "This is a wonderful and rare cloth. Where did you get it?"

"My granddaughter wove it," the old man answered.

"Then let her weave more. I will pay you well," said the lord. He gave many coins and treasures to the old man.

The old man was surprised that the cloth was so valuable. He bought many presents in town and brought the bundles home.

The old woman opened the first bundle; she found rice—very good rice—in it. "We always eat millet except on New Year's Day. What a surprise! Now I'll make some rice balls," the old woman said.

Then she opened the second bundle; she found wooden clogs, combs, and thread. In the third one she found dried fish, beans, and raw sugar.

The old man pulled out a sack from the bottom of the bundles. The old woman opened it. She found many gold coins. The girl looked happily at the rejoicing faces of the old man and woman.

"All of this we owe to you. We cannot thank you enough," said the old man and woman to her.

The girl kept weaving every day.

The old man took the cloth to the lord. Each time the lord rewarded him with many gold coins, and the old man and woman grew more and more wealthy. Now they slept on cotton mattresses instead of straw ones. They used ivory chopsticks instead of wooden ones. They ate good rice instead of millet. They lived in a fine mansion.

A year passed. The girl continued to weave, but she became thinner and thinner and grew weaker and weaker. The old man and woman were very concerned about her.

One day the old woman said to the old man, "I am worried. The sound of the loom has become timid and faint. Maybe she is sick. Should we look inside once?"

"No, we cannot," said the old man. "We promised we would not."

The girl grew weaker and weaker day by day. At last the old woman could not stand it anymore. She peeked behind the screen.

"Look," she whispered to the old man. "A big white crane!"

They saw the cranc pull one of her own feathers and weave it with the silk threads. Her feathers were almost all gone. The old man and woman burst into tears and hurried away.

After a while, the girl came out from behind the screen quietly. Her eyes were filled with tears.

"Grandmother, Grandfather, I am the crane that was dying in the trap that snowy day."

"The big white crane," the old man uttered.

"I've been working for you to repay you for your kindness. But once my true figure is seen, I have to be the crane again forever and return to the sky."

"Forgive me," the old woman said.

"Don't leave us," the old man pleaded.

The old man and woman cried and cried as the girl went out of the door.

The girl said, "Grandmother, Grandfather, thank you for loving me. I pray for your health and happiness forever." As soon as she finished saying this, she turned into the big white crane.

The old man and woman stood near some blue moonflowers blooming in the sunset. They watched the beautiful, graceful crane soar into the sky and then melt out of sight.

The Disappearing Island

Adapted from one of the many old Celtic legends
by Pat Clyne

Long before there ever was a St. Patrick's Day, a young boy named Robby O'Nire lived with his mother on a small farm near the blue-green sea.

One day Robby was out searching for wood when he heard faint cries. At first he thought it was only a sea gull flying overhead, but when he looked up, there were no birds in sight. Then he knew the cries were coming from somewhere out at sea.

Robby raced to the water's edge. When he got there, he could see a small boat caught on the rocks out in the water. The sea was boiling and pounding against the wooden boat, and an old woman inside it was calling for help.

She cried, "Please save me!"

"It's the Old Woman of the Cove," Robby said to himself. Then he looked around for someone to help the old woman. However, it was late in the afternoon and the beach was deserted.

"Help me or I will drown. I cannot swim!" came the old woman's frightened voice.

How could he save her? He was only a boy. He had no boat. And he did not think he was strong enough to swim through the raging surf. Even if he were strong enough, would he dare to risk his life for this old woman? After all, almost everybody called her a witch.

Of course, his mother said the Old Woman of the Cove was not a witch. It was just that she lived all alone and told strange stories.

But if he tried to save her, he might be swallowed up in the waves. Then there would be no one to take care of his mother, no one to take care of their farm. Still, he knew he could not stand there and watch the old woman drown.

"Oh, please help me!" the old woman called again and again.

"I'll help you!" Robby shouted suddenly. Just as he did so, he saw a coil of rope near some fishing nets drying on the sand.

He tried throwing the rope to the old woman, but she was too far away. Then he noticed there was a short time between waves when the sea was fairly quiet. If he could swim to the boat during those few minutes, then he could use the rope to pull himself and the old woman back to the shore. He knew he could not swim and hold her at the same time.

Robby quickly tied one end of the rope to a rock on the beach and the other end around his waist. He waited for just the right time. Then he plunged into the water and swam to the sinking boat. He grabbed the old woman's hand.

"Hold on to me!" he cried.

Pulling and panting, Robby struggled to reach the shore. When they finally got there, Robby helped the Old Woman of the Cove find a place to sit. Then he waited until she caught her breath.

As he did so, Robby looked out over the sea to the emerald-green island in the distance. How he wished he could live on that island, where the land was rich and lovely. It was not at all like the tiny farm where he and his mother grew just enough food for the two of them to eat.

But the island was said to be enchanted. Some people had tried to live on the island, but every time they did, the whole island would suddenly disappear beneath the waves. Then, after a few days, the island would begin to rise again—lush, green, and inviting.

"Do you like that beautiful disappearing island, young Robby O'Nire?"

Robby jumped in surprise at the words of the Old Woman of the Cove.

"How did you know my name?" the boy asked.

"I know many things," the old woman answered. "I know that you are a very brave lad, and I must reward you for saving my life."

Before Robby could reply that he did not want any reward, the old woman went on. "Because you were brave enough to rescue me from the sea, I am going to tell you a secret—one that can bring you much happiness."

"What is it?" Robby asked excitedly.

"The secret of how to keep that island from disappearing beneath the sea. Once you know that, you can go to live there. That is what you would like to do, isn't it?"

Robby was so amazed he could only nod his head and take a deep breath.

"It is true that the island is enchanted," the Old Woman of the Cove went on. "But the spell can be broken by placing a sword of iron in the exact center of the island. It must be done quickly, though. For the island will begin to sink the minute you set foot on it."

"But how can I get there?" Robby asked. "My mother and I are poor. We do not own a boat. And how will I find the exact center of the island?"

The Old Woman of the Cove smiled at him. "There is a giant oak tree right at the center. It is taller than any other on the island. As for the boat, I have another at my home on the cove. If you are as brave as I think you are, you will come there bright and early in the morning."

Robby didn't really think he was very brave, but early the next morning he was at the home of the Old Woman of the Cove.

The old woman did not seem surprised. It was almost as if she knew he would come. "Here," she said, handing him a sword made of iron. "Bury this iron sword in the ground at the center of the island. Once you do so, the island will never again sink beneath the sea. But remember, you must hurry, Robby O'Nire!"

Robby did hurry, for as soon as he set foot on the island, it began to sink. It was a foggy morning, and he was afraid he would not find the oak tree in time. In fact, he almost got back into the boat.

Then he remembered how much he wanted to live on this beautiful island. Here his mother would not have to work so hard, and there would be plenty of grass for their cow to eat.

The water was lapping against his ankles when Robby finally found the great oak tree. With trembling fingers, he pushed the iron sword into the earth. Then he took a rock and hammered the sword all the way down, out of sight.

As soon as this was done, the island began to rise, and it never again disappeared beneath the sea.

Down through the years, the story was repeated of how brave Robby O'Nire buried the iron sword. It is but one of the many legends about the island we know as Ireland.

Wisdom and Li Ming

A Chinese fable retold
by Dorothy L. Allen

Three frightened mandarins hid behind a single tiny rosebush. Courtiers fell upon their chins and prayed that soft words might prevail. The most dignified, wisest teacher bowed to the floor and waited for the fierce words of the emperor to fall.

"My son, the heir to all I have! Look at him!" the emperor demanded.

The teacher lifted his head and opened one eye. Li Ming, son of the most wonderful emperor, was looking out the window at the birds in the tree.

"Oh, most undignified man! Do you call yourself a teacher?"

The kneeling man trembled.

"Why can't you teach my son to be wise? He answers the most simple questions with nonsense. Listen! Just listen."

Li Ming smiled at his father. "Oh, yes, most high father. Do you have a question to ask me?"

"Just one," the emperor replied. "Which is closer, Shanghai or the moon?"

This was an easy question because Shanghai was only a few hundred miles from the imperial palace.

"The moon is closer," Li Ming answered.

"The moon!" the emperor raged. "Why do you say that?"

"Because," the boy answered calmly, "I can see the moon, but I cannot see Shanghai."

"You, who call yourself a teacher, I will give you two weeks to teach this boy something. I have invited many guests to my castle to meet the prince. You must teach him. Now begone!"

Every day for two weeks the teacher explained to the prince, "Shanghai is closer. Even though you can see the moon, Shanghai is closer."

At last, on the day before the guests were to arrive, the teacher called to the prince, "Which is closer, Shanghai or the moon?"

"Shanghai is closer," the prince answered, and the teacher was happy.

The crowd had gathered in the big hall to greet the emperor. There were fine gifts of gold and rare jade. When all the gifts had been presented, the ruler called his son forward.

"My son, I have invited all my subjects to meet you. I have invited guests from everywhere. I want them to know how clever you are. One day when the kingdom is yours, they must know that they have a wise ruler. Now, my son, tell me, which is closer, Shanghai or the moon?"

"Shanghai, my father," Li Ming said.

"Very good, my son. Now please tell me how you know this is true."

Poor Li Ming! His teacher had not told him why. He must answer his father, or the emperor would grow angry in front of everyone.

"Well, come now," the emperor coaxed. "Tell me how you know this is true."

"Because," the boy answered after some thought, "I know you have invited guests from everywhere."

"Yes, that is right," the emperor said impatiently. "But what does that have to do with my question?"

"Because," the Prince said, "I can see the people from Shanghai are here, but the people from the moon have not yet arrived."

What Size Is Kindness?

An African folktale retold
by Josepha Sherman

Long ago, in the days when animals and people could speak to each other, a hunter set out with his bow and arrows to find game. He heard a strange sound and stopped to listen.

There it was again, a dry little, scratchy little sound. And ever so quietly, it was coming from a hole in the ground.

What was making the sound? It was a cane rat, a scrawny, ugly little cane rat that had fallen into the hole and couldn't climb out.

"Help me!" it begged the hunter. "Please, kind man, help me out of this hole!"

The hunter lowered his bow into the hole, and the cane rat eagerly scrambled up the bow and out of the hole.

"Thank you," said the cane rat. "I would have starved down there. Kind man, if I can ever help you, I will."

The hunter laughed. "What, you help me? A funny little thing like you?"

"We shall see," said the cane rat. And with a nod of his head, he scurried off.

Grinning, the hunter went on his way, too. But he hadn't gone far before the wind began to rise and great storm clouds began tumbling overhead.

"I'd better find shelter," he said.

The hunter hurried into a cave to wait for the rain to stop. He settled down to eat the food he had brought with him.

Suddenly a shadow darkened the mouth of the cave as a huge lion came bounding in. The hunter tried to grab his bow, but the lion blocked his way. He was trapped!

"Ah . . . good day to you, lion," said the hunter politely. "Is this your cave? I didn't mean to take it from you. I was only waiting for the rain to stop. So now, if you'll step aside, I'll be on my way and—"

"No!" roared the lion. "Stay! Eat your meal, man. And then I will eat *you!*"

The hunter thought, "This is surely the end of me. But then there came a laugh, a laugh that echoed through the cave. "Oh, yes!" boomed a great and terrible voice. "The hunter will eat his meal. The lion will eat the hunter. Then I will eat the lion!"

"Where are you?" snarled the lion.

"All around you!"

"Who are you?"

The mighty laugh rang all through the cave. "I am the terrible slayer of lions! Hurry, lion, eat the hunter, so that I may eat you!"

The lion hesitated. "I—I don't think I'm very hungry now," he muttered. And he turned and ran out of that cave, ran just like a frightened cub, until he was out of sight.

The hunter snatched up his bow. Who was this terrible slayer of lions? "Who could be fearsome enough to frighten away a lion?" he whispered.

"I could," said the cane rat, stepping out from behind a rock.

"But you're only a scrawny little cane rat!" the hunter said. "Who had that terrible voice?"

"I did," said the cane rat modestly. "I know I am too small to fight the lion, but the wonderful echoes in this cave made even my little voice sound great and powerful."

The hunter laughed. "Oh, my clever friend, forgive me. You may be small, but I should have realized that cleverness and kindness know no size."

The Legend of the Red Bird

A Cherokee tale retold
by Bonnie Highsmith Taylor

In the First Times, everything had life. Wind, fog, rain, shadows—even sunbeams.

One Sun Child, as sunbeams were called, loved going into the mountain forests where the Cherokee children played.

Sometimes Father Sun would say to this Sun Child, "Today you shall spread your rays across the prairie." Or, "This is a good day for you to go into the deep canyon where the great river runs and the fish frolic and play."

But Sun Child would beg, "Oh, please, Father, let me go to the forest. It is so dark there. The children need my light."

Father Sun would always give in.

Nearly every day in the springtime Sun Child warmed the young flowers that bloomed in the woods. He wakened the ladybugs from their winter sleep. He listened to the laughter of the children.

In the summer Sun Child danced with the butterflies. He sparkled on the ripples of small streams where the children cooled their feet. He was happiest in the summer, for he could come to the forest every single day.

In the autumn, Sun Child raced with the red and gold leaves as they made their way, twirling and fluttering, to the ground. He warmed the children's chilly fingers and noses in the cool mornings.

But when winter came, Sun Child was sad, for only once in a while could he go to the forest and watch the children play.

Father Sun tried to explain. "You must be patient. The Fog Children, the Wind Children, and the Snow Children must have their turns."

"But in the winter the flowers do not bloom," cried Sun Child. "All the birds leave and go to the warm south. The forest is dark and gloomy. The children need me to brighten the cold winter days. He sighed. "I wish I could stay in the forest always."

"You shall have your wish," said Father Sun.

Suddenly the Sun Child found himself in the forest. But what was this? He was covered with feathers, beautiful red feathers. They glistened on his wings and rose in a handsome crest on his head. He was a bird!

Now he could stay in the forest always. When the other birds flew south for the winter, he would stay behind to brighten the forest. And no one would ever know that this red bird, the cardinal, was once a sunbeam.